UPON
THE SANDS
OF
TIME

UPON
THE SANDS
OF
TIME

DIANE SWAFFIELD

The Elonias Foundation

Chapter 1

Upon the Sands of Time

As I stood outside of the Temple, I took a deep breath and looked up into the clear night sky. The darkness of the night was illumined by the stars that could be seen, oh so clearly. The moon was absent and all was so still, and so silent.

It wasn't long before they came. In the silence of the night, they entered back into view. Two of them, dressed as usual in garments of light that radiated so brightly against the blackness of the night.

I raised my hand to greet them, as I moved swiftly towards them with my bare feet not making a sound on the desert sands. Time stood still, as my mind wandered back to the moment I first saw them ...

''Hurry up!'' The words echoed through the valley, as I struggled to walk up the steep slope.

At the tender age of 10 years, I was finding it hard to keep up with my brother, who was four years older, and who kept reminding me that I was far too slow.

My heart was pounding in my chest as I finally made my way to where he was impatiently waiting. "I can't go another step further," I said. "I am just too tired."

Anger crossed his face as he spoke. "I can't wait here with you until you are rested, I will just have to go on alone. I will be back for you as soon as I am able." And with that, he was gone. His long legs striding up the pathway, until he was soon out of sight.

It was a very warm day, and I was happy to be left alone. The view into the valley, as always, was especially beautiful, but today it seemed more so now that the rest of the day was mine to spend how I wished.

I lay back in the grass and closed my eyes, but I must have fallen asleep, for I was suddenly startled to hear my name being called. "Amoen, Amoen, wake up."

I sat up and looked around, but could see no-one. Again, I heard my name, "Amoen, Amoen." I rose to my feet and looked around to see where it was coming from, and there, just behind me, stood two figures that were oh so tall, and seemed to be made of light.

They smiled at me and said, "Amoen, we need to tell you something ..."

There is always a time when you just can't find the right words, and this was the time. All I could think to say was, "How do you know my name?"

The one closest to me smiled and said, "We have always known you, and your name is only a name within this moment of your time, but it is not in ours. Amoen, there is a journey that we need you to make, and we need you to make it now."

I stared at them in utter bewilderment. "But I am only a young boy, what do you want with me? I can't go anywhere with you, as my brother told me to wait here for him. He will be returning on nightfall, and will be most concerned for my safety if I am gone."

With that explanation out of the way, surely they would understand the predicament I was in. Didn't they know that my brother Daniel had a terrible temper, and would be so angry to find me gone? If they knew Daniel like they said they knew me, then they would have to understand.

It was at that moment, that I knew something was wrong, very, very wrong. The ground under my feet seemed to give way, and I seemed to be spinning, around and around. I don't know what happened, but I don't remember anything else until I opened my eyes to find myself lying on the floor of a room that was brightly lit, from walls that seemed to be made of light.

I sat up and looked around. I was in a large room, larger than any room I had ever seen before, and the air was warm with a strange, sweet smell, and I was alone, totally alone.

I have to admit I felt very afraid of what might come next. I felt totally confused. How did I get here, and for what reason? I remember lying on the grassy slopes of the mountain overlooking the valley where I lived, and then those two people came and spoke to me about going on a journey ...

My thoughts were suddenly interrupted by the sound of a door opening. At the far end of the room, the door opened and the two people who spoke to me on the mountain entered.

I must have sounded very angry because I remember shouting, "Why have you brought me here? I told you I didn't want to go anywhere!"

"You haven't gone anywhere. That is the point," one of them said. "You are still upon the side of the mountain. In fact you are asleep."

I tried to understand what he was saying. "If I am asleep, then this must be a dream," I replied.

"Not at all, for this is what is real, and where you are is a dream," he replied.

"Life is a dream, but within that dream, that what is real may enter in. We have brought you here to show you the content of the dream and how to identify when the real has entered, so that your pathway through your life can be understood more fully."

"I am only young," I said. "Why did you not choose my brother, who is much older than I to share this insight with?"

"Your brother is a character within the dream, whilst you are not.

Your age is only an image of identification of your response within the dream, but yet this image does not share with you the complete recognition that age is of no consequence, but instead your image of it is.

The journey to which you are taking is two-fold. To relinquish the past is to permit the future to begin.

However, within the possibility of the future never being given to you, then how will your journey begin and how will your journey end? For surely the future determines who you have been, and how you will proceed from that point is dependent upon the future becoming the past."

My teachers at school always told me that I was not very bright, and I was starting to believe them. I did not understand anything that I was being told. Absolutely nothing! They had obviously made a mistake, and confused me with someone else. As if reading my thoughts, the one that had spoken before, spoke up again.

"You will not understand what we are saying, but that is why we have brought you here, so as to show you and explain more fully what your life will bring. Time does not exist here, so we can take as long as you need. Do not worry, for when your brother Daniel returns, you will be there, waiting for him, as if you had never been anywhere."

You can't imagine how that very statement took away all of my worry and concern. It's not as if I was afraid of my brother, but I didn't want to upset him by finding me gone.

I really believed in that moment that I was dreaming all of this, and somehow these strange people were really my characters in my dream.

I laughed at the thought of mentioning it to them, but then I had never had a dream like this one, and I didn't want to spoil it. I wonder what I could dream up next?

"This room is an aspect of your mind. And within that aspect, there are many things to discover about yourself. Look around you and tell us what you see."

I did as he asked, and looked around the room, not wanting to miss anything. I took a moment to explore my surroundings.

The walls seemed to be made of light. The ceiling was very high and looked to be made of sandstone. The stone floor was uneven in parts, and was obviously not made by the best stone cutter. The room was empty, except for a long table at the far end, near the door. Apart from these observations, there was nothing else to tell them.

"Look again, Amoen, for you have surely missed something." I was a little puzzled by this remark, for I was very careful in not missing one detail, for I prided myself with my ability to notice and remember things.

"No, I believe I have told you all that I have seen," I replied.

"The power of the mind can deceive you, Amoen," he replied. "When you are able to know the power that you have, then you will know what you have missed. We will now take the first step in helping you understand this fact."

With that statement hardly finished, everything around me changed. The room disappeared, and in its place we were standing once again on the side of the Mountain, overlooking the valley, where I first met them. To my utter amazement and surprise, I saw myself sleeping soundly, just as I had been told earlier.

"Look carefully, Amoen, at yourself sleeping. Which one of you is real? Is it you who stands here, or is it the one sleeping? Whilst you stand here and believe it is 'you' who is real, then the one sleeping is not. However, if we were to awaken the one sleeping and ask the same question, then what do you think would be the answer? I believe we will find out."

And with that he stepped forward to 'the other me' sleeping and gently touched 'me'. The effect was instantaneous. I woke up, and I became aware of being in two places at once.

The most amazing thing was that I became two people. I experienced feeling frightened by seeing myself with these two 'light' people, and I also felt totally confused at seeing myself looking back at me. How could I be in two places at once? It was impossible, but it was happening.

"Amoen (speaking to the 'me' he had just awoken), you need to come with us, for we have something to show you ..."

I stood up and rubbed my eyes. I just couldn't believe what I was seeing. If you have ever had the shock of being woken up and confronted by yourself, then you would know what I mean.

There was an eerie silence, as I stood looking at the figure that so resembled myself … and yet, was all this a dream?

The silence was shattered by my name being called.

"Amoen, we need you to come with us, for we have a journey to undertake."

"I can't come with you," I replied. "For I am awaiting my brother, who is to return upon nightfall, and if I am not here, he will be concerned for my whereabouts."

As I listened to him speaking, it became all too much for me to bear. "What do you want of me?" I cried. "What is happening? Let it stop now!" My words were uttered with sheer desperation, so as to hold onto any sense of reality.

Thank goodness my brain rushed to my aid immediately. It was a dream, remember, it is only a dream! Relief flooded through me as I grasped onto that thought. Of course, I had forgotten, for all looked and seemed so real for a moment. It was obvious that I needed to take hold of this dream and change the content immediately, so that all confusion ceased.

Chapter 2

I stared at him in disbelief. He was actually yelling at the top of his voice, and he sounded just like me!

His face was flushed with what seemed to be a combination of rage and fear, but then it all subsided, and he actually smiled! This surely could not be happening, it must be a dream, and that being the case, I hoped that it would soon end.

The two beings of light looked at both of us, and then asked, "Which one of you is real, and which one is the character within the dream?"

"I am," I replied, "for you have just awoken me, as I lay sleeping."

"No, that is not true," I replied, "for surely it is I who is real, for I remember being taken away from here to a room, to which you asked me to describe, and now I find myself back here again. It is surely I who is real, and he is the character in the dream."

...

It was at that point that everything changed again, and I found myself back in the room. Thank goodness there was only one of me. "Why did you need to show me myself??" I asked.

"To share with you the reality and illusionary aspect through your mind of who you believe you are," was the reply.

"To belong to one space and one time is only a limited image of self. To allow one to view another aspect of ones being through an individualised thought is to understand that what seems real is quite often the opposite. Who you believe you are could be the memory of who you might have been. However, when you recognise as to which 'you' is real, then all alters. All is different, completely."

I wish I could say at this point that I became all know-ing, and everything that was told to me became so very clear. However, that was not the case, and I was even more confused than ever.

"Let us go back, Amoen, to the place where you first saw us, but is not the first place that we met you, at all." The scene changed, and again we were back to the side of the Mountain, where I was sleeping.

"We will do it again, Amoen, but this time with a difference. Just watch and say nothing, nothing at all!"

I did as he requested, and stood silently, watching and won-dering what he meant. What did he mean when he said that it was not the first time that we had met?

I did not remember seeing either of them before, and if I had done so, I would surely not be standing here, still unsure as to who they were, and what they wanted with me.

Oh well, this dream has become stranger and stranger. A thought suddenly occurred to me. What if I was to dream that I was the one sleeping. That would surely trick them.

I closed my eyes, and concentrated very, very hard, imagining myself lying down in the grass, and feeling very sleepy. That would surely create a twist in this dream.

It must have worked, because the next moment, I heard someone calling my name. "Amoen, Amoen, wake up." I opened my eyes to see ...

Oh no! What had happened? The Mountain had gone, and in its place was a small room, sparsely furnished with only a chair and a small table beside it. I seemed to be lying on a woven mat on a stone floor.

My eyes beheld a young man, standing over me, who looked extremely concerned. "Wake up Amoen, you will be late!"

I sat up, and it was then that I realised that I was no longer a young boy, but instead I was a man! "Where am I?" I asked.

"Amoen, are you not well?" was his worried reply.

"You are in the Temple of Remembrance, surely you remember that!"

Chapter 3

The sun was warm upon my face, as I opened my eyes to the beautiful view of the valley below. I felt a little stiff, as if I had been asleep for a long time, and yet the sun was still high in the sky. I recalled a dream that I had had. A most unusual dream. Two men had come and awoken me, and then I laughed to myself.

I remember that there were two of me. The 'me' that they had woken up, and the other 'me' who stood with those two men. And there was something else: what was it? Oh yes, I remember. They said that they needed me to go on a journey with them, but I don't remember whether I went with them or not. What a strange dream!

I was starting to feel thirsty and a little hungry. I had already eaten the food that Mother had prepared for me, and the water bottle was already empty. The climb had taken its toll, and I had long since drank the last drop. I felt cross with myself for not asking Daniel to exchange his water bottle with mine. He could have filled the empty bottle when he came to the stream, that I knew to be further up the mountain.

I stood there, trying to make up my mind as to whether I would make my way up the mountain to the stream, or find some shelter away from the sun, and wait for Daniel to come back down the trail.

The thought of climbing again was far too much to bear, and so the obvious choice was to head towards the clump of trees in the distance and make myself comfortable in the shade. Yes that is what I will do.

Perhaps there are some berry bushes there, and if so, then I can fill my belly and quench my thirst at the same time. The very thought made me feel much better, and so I headed off in the direction of the dense timberland.

I was never any good at judging distance, and I found that the timberland was much further away than I thought. I felt tired and miserable, and vowed at that moment never to be left behind again, but my sense of despair and frustration quickly changed as my adventurous nature rose to the surface. A cave! I had discovered a cave!

As I stood at its entrance I felt a feeling of trepidation envelop me. A feeling that I could not explain at all. My original excitement at discovering the cave quickly changed to a feeling of unsureness as to whether I should enter inside or not. I took a few steps backwards to review the situation.

I do not know how long I stood there, debating as to whether I should investigate the cave or not, but I became aware that the sun was becoming very hot on my back.

Don't be silly, I scolded myself, for surely the cave would be so much cooler. What if I did not venture too far inside, but instead just rested away from the hot sun within the cave's entrance?

I quickly became cross with myself. I had never felt this way before. What would my friends think of me if I told them that I was afraid to enter a silly cave? The thought of that became too much to bear, and so I took a deep breath and entered.

The bright light of the sun was such a contrast to the darkness of the cave. My eyes took some time to adjust, and I had to admit, it certainly was much cooler in here. Perhaps it was the sun that had affected me, and caused my earlier feelings of unsureness. Yes, that was it! I was not afraid of anything!!

A surge of confidence from that very thought challenged me to go further into the cave than I had earlier intended. I found myself taking long strides, almost as if to prove to myself that my feeling of cowardice was a temporary feeling due to the hot midday sun and my lack of water.

As usual, my determination to prove myself took me straight into trouble. I suddenly lost my footing as the cave floor dropped sharply, and I found myself tumbling down a steep incline that seemed to go forever. I don't know whether the journey down the incline was the most painful or the sudden landing at the bottom.

Whatever .. the result was that my whole body was racked with pain from the ordeal, and I became angry with myself for not watching where I was going.

As I stood up and looked around me, I found that I had fallen into a very large cavern. There were two lamps, burning brightly. They were placed upon a large stone slab, alongside a large tumbler, which much to my surprise, held what appeared to be clear fresh water.

My thirst was so great that I did not even give a thought that the water could be in any way contaminated. However, as the first drop touched my lips, I realised that something was wrong. The last thing I remember was the ground coming up to meet me ..

Chapter 4

"Amoen, Amoen, hurry, hurry!" I was startled by the urgency in the sound of his voice. A young man appeared in the doorway, beckoning me to follow him.

"You can't be late Amoen, for He is awaiting us. Come quickly!"

I did as he asked, and followed him down a long passageway that led to a flight of stairs. He was moving at such a fast pace that I was afraid that he would soon disappear from view. At this point, I realised that in order to find out what was happening to me, I had better hurry and keep up with him.

Our journey was quickly halted as we arrived at a large door. My companion knocked twice upon the door and waited.

The door opened almost immediately by a young man, whose beauty almost took my breath away. His hair was golden, and hung loosely around his shoulders. His eyes were so blue, they reminded me of the sky on a clear day.

"Come in, Amoen" he said. "We have been awaiting you." With those words spoken, my companion quickly turned and walked away, leaving me to enter the room alone.

What a dream! I thought to myself, and I laughed inwardly at the need to create such a dream. Here I was, all grown up, dressed up like a holy man, and being confronted by someone with golden hair and blue eyes.

What imagination I had!! I just hoped that I could remember all of this when I woke up, for I could tell many a tale to my friends and keep them amused for a long, long time.

I took a step into the next part of my dream ...

...

Voices, I could hear voices. They seemed so distant as I drifted into and out of consciousness.

Then clearly, I heard a voice .. "Amoen, Amoen, open your eyes." I did as I was instructed, and was completely amazed by what I saw. The cave was gone, and in its place was a large room with walls that seemed to be made of light.

Two men stood before me. One with golden hair and the other's hair was dark. Both were dressed in long white gowns that seemed to be made of silk. Golden threads had been woven through the fabric, and as they moved towards me, their gowns shimmered in the light.

The one with the golden hair knelt down in front of me and said. "Amoen, you are wondering why we have brought you here, but we need to show you something. Very soon, a young man will enter through that door at the end of the room and he will become a little distressed when he sees you.

We want you to know something, and that is we have brought you here to help him understand something. It is very important that you listen very carefully to what we are going to tell him, because one day you will need to remember it."

My thoughts were racing through my mind. I knew that I should not have entered that cave. It was the fall and then when I drank that water .. surely it was all too much. My body must have just dropped off to sleep.

Yes, that is what happened. I surely must be dreaming this. What a relief!! I will just go along with it all, and then I will find myself awake in the cave again. But what if this wasn't a dream? It was then that I felt a little uneasy. What if my brother had already returned and was looking for me .. he would not think of looking for me in the cave. Perhaps it was already nightfall.

My wild thoughts were interrupted by someone knocking on the door. The one with the golden hair opened the door and a few moments later a young man entered. He was dressed in a simple white robe, tied at the waist by a golden cord. His feet were bare. He seemed familiar somehow. He looked around the room, then his gaze met mine.

If time found a way to meet itself, it was then, in that very moment, that it happened.

The young boy, that I am, was looking intently at who he had become. But what about the years in between?

What had become of them? I stood transfixed with that very recognition. The past and future had met, and yet what had happened in between the two to allow both to exist?

It was as if something had sliced time in half and taken a giant piece from it, almost as if it had never happened.

And with that thought, the one with the golden hair turned to me and said quietly, "Amoen, what you are viewing is yourself within the young boy, and yet you are also occupying the time of the future.

What exists in between has not happened as yet. For time reveals nothing but itself over and over again. But when the past is not to connect to the future, as it has always done, then that what connects it to itself must be broken.

For you have entered the Temple of Remembrance once again, within the future of the young boy. What I need to tell you is very simple, but yet you need to listen very carefully to what I am about to reveal.

Opposites attract the ratio of the past back into itself. The need to know is always offset by the need to not know. The need to love is always offset by the need to not love, and so on. One cannot move through time without understanding the law of opposites."

I nodded my head, almost as a measure of an expected response, and yet somewhere within me I understood what he was saying. As the young boy I felt awkward and afraid, and yet I portrayed to myself a feeling of extreme fearlessness, so as to prove that I could measure up to my older brother and to my friends.

As the person that I had become, I knew I had not changed, for the unsureness had followed me into the future. The only difference was that I now had to face that unsureness within the Temple of Remembrance within the future.

"That is where you are wrong, Amoen" he said, interrupting my thoughts. "For within the future of the past you have found yourself once again within the Temple of Remembrance.

However, within the 'new' future, you will not. For you will be someone entirely different, with a different perspective to yourself and all around you. The Temple of Remembrance will not be a place where you will be, but instead you will find yourself within a far distant Land that will offer to you so many things, as yet untold of.

Whilst your vision is within the small boy, you will view the future with possibilities, but as the young man, there was only one possibility that you took, which obviously led you to where you are now.

The relevant action leads to the relevant result. But if you were to alter even one action, then the result will lead you into a different possibility altogether. The purpose to life can be likened to an array of possibilities, with each one aligning itself to its opposite."

My mind was reeling with so many thoughts. How was it possible to change the future? What possibility led me to the place that he described? What did it all mean?

So many questions!

The one with the dark hair, whom had kept so very silent, stepped forward and spoke to the 'older me'.

"Your journey is now finished. We will not need you to remain here with us. For you are not 'real', but only an echo of a possibility."

If I hadn't seen it with my very eyes, I wouldn't have believed it. But that young man just vanished. He disappeared, as if he had never been there. Who were these two strange men? If they could make him disappear, what if they made me disappear too? I gulped at the prospect of never being seen again. Lost .. gone forever!

The one with the dark hair turned to me and said, "Amoen, do not feel afraid, for upon this day you have entered the Temple of Remembrance. We have brought you here to introduce you to what that means.

For we cannot allow you to enter the future as the young man that you have just seen, but instead we need you to enter into a place where all will be revealed to you. Come, come with me and we will show you many, many things."

I did not understand at that moment, that my life would change so drastically. But what happened then has altered the course of my life and the life of many others.

As the young boy I was unable to view the power of what was to come.

I did not realise then the importance of seeing myself iin the future, and how important it was that I did not reach maturity with the same values and feelings that I carried on that day.

The young boy, on that day, was oblivious to the role that he was to play in the future.

Looking back now, I recognise that the Temple of Remembrance is the only entry point into what is 'real'. All else is only an image of what is possible. The 'real' journey started upon that day.

...

The sands felt soft under my feet. And their greeting was as warm as it had always been. But something was different, and before I even had an opportunity to ask .. I heard the words that I had been wanting and yet not wanting to hear .. "It is time to wake up Amoen."

I opened my eyes to see the sun disappearing from view. The night air was descending and I felt the cool wind entering my body that had just wakened from sleep. All seemed so different somehow.

I felt that I had slept for such a long, long time. I felt dazed, almost as if my mind was full of something that I needed to remember. A dream .. yes, I had had a dream. A strange and yet wonderful dream.

***

A young child with such a limited perception of what had happened to him stood on the mountain that day. And yet within that child something was taking place. Many would call it 'a stirring within'. Nothing could ever be the same again. And nothing was.

A cycle of events, that one calls destiny, suddenly changed direction, and an opportunity was born for something completely new to exist within his life. What was new was his need to be different. To no longer have the unsureness of his past, and to move towards a different future than the one that he had witnessed he had become.

To isolate the past within the power of memory, is indeed empowering the need to hold onto the memory. But if the memory of the past is no longer the power point to one's next thought, then the power of memory, attached to the past, loses its need to be the focus of ones next thought or even action.

This was certainly not the conscious recognition of a young boy on that day, but as a young man in his new future, he would ponder and promote this understanding through all of his thoughts and actions.

THE END

Was that really the end of the story? Or perhaps it was the beginning. It is up to the reader to decide.

Perhaps you have had a dream. A dream like Amoen's. whereby you can see yourself in the future, being no different than you are today. To some, it is a nightmare, but to others, a relief.

The sameness can be a comfort or it can be a curse. It depends upon whether you see your dream as a new beginning or the end.

To the reader who views their dream as a relief, then there is no need to read on. Your story has finished. But to the others who see their dream as a new beginning, then this is your story. This is the beginning of the 'real' story ...

The sound of laughter echoed through the valley.

I sat upright in my bed wondering who was so full of joy, especially when the sun had only just penetrated the darkness from the night that had just departed. I listened intently, but the laughter had disappeared and the silence of the morning had now taken its place.

The beauty of that silence convinced me to not go back to sleep, but instead to take the opportunity to venture outside, for when the sun first shines its rays across the valley, was, for me, the most beautiful time of all.

I quickly dressed and made my way outside.

All seemed so still except for a gentle breeze that brought with it the fragrance of the first flowers of Spring. To awaken to the silence of the early morning brought to me a joy that I could not explain.

The rays of the sun started to penetrate the shadows that were left over from the night. All around me glowed with the promise of a new day.

Yesterday seemed a long way away as I tried to retrieve what yesterday had shown to me.

The power of all of my yesterdays had certainly brought to me the beginning of this new day, but yet beyond this thought I knew that this day was different.

This day was the real beginning, for it held the promise of all that could be new, all that I had not as yet revealed to be real. For within that moment I knew that yesterday had never existed.

That was the paradox to life. If we did not live within our yesterdays, then only today would exist.

Within that thought, within that knowing, I knew my life had only just begun.

That is all.

THE REAL END

WITHIN THE PAST
LIES OUR FUTURE.

WITHIN THE FUTURE
LIES OUR PAST.

HOWEVER, IF THE
PAST DOES NOT ALLOW
THE FUTURE TO BEGIN,
THEN ALL IS NEW.

Available Reading:

**The Journey Home
with Elonias**
Diane Swaffield

The Greatest Story Never Told
Amoen, Diane Swaffield

The Temple of Remembrance
Diane Swaffield

A Life Worth Living
Diane Swaffield

Available Viewing:

'The Illusion of Reality' Documentary
Written, produced & Narrated by Jason Swaffield

Online Resources:

eloniasfoundation.com
thetimecentre.com